CTPC

This Walker book belongs to:

· ·

· ·

· ·

For Lisa, the Brave

B. B.

To Sonny

K. M. D.

First published 2010 by Walker Books Ltd
87 Vauxhall Walk, London SE11 5HJ

This edition published 2011

2 4 6 8 10 9 7 5 3 1

Text © 2010 Bonny Becker
Illustrations © 2010 Kady MacDonald Denton

The right of Bonny Becker and Kady MacDonald Denton to be identified as
author and illustrator respectively of this work has been asserted by them
in accordance with the Copyright, Designs and Patents Act 1988

This book has been typeset in New Baskerville

Printed in China

British Library Cataloguing in Publication Data:
a catalogue record for this book is available from the British Library

ISBN 978-1-4063-3205-6

www.walker.co.uk

A Bedtime for Bear

Bonny Becker

illustrated by

Kady MacDonald Denton

WALKER BOOKS
AND SUBSIDIARIES
LONDON · BOSTON · SYDNEY · AUCKLAND

Everything had to be just so for Bear's bedtime.

His glass of water had to sit on exactly the right spot on his bed stand.

His favourite pillow had to be nicely fluffed up.

His nightcap needed to fit snugly on his head.

Most of all, it had to be quiet – very, very quiet.

One evening Bear heard a *tap, tap, tapping* on his front door.

When he opened the door, there stood Mouse, small and grey and bright-eyed.

He clasped a tiny suitcase in his paw.

"I am here to spend the night!" exclaimed Mouse with a happy wiggle of his whiskers.

"Surely we agreed on next Tuesday," protested Bear.

"No," said Mouse. "You most definitely said tonight."

"Oh," said Bear.

Bear had never had an overnight guest before. Guests could quite possibly mess things up and make a noise, and Bear needed quiet, absolute quiet, at bedtime.

Even so, Bear and Mouse enjoyed an evening playing draughts and drinking warm cocoa, and soon it was time for bed.

"Remember, I must have absolute quiet," said Bear.

"Oh, indeed," said Mouse.

Bear set out his glass of water,

adjusted his nightcap,

fluffed up his favourite pillow

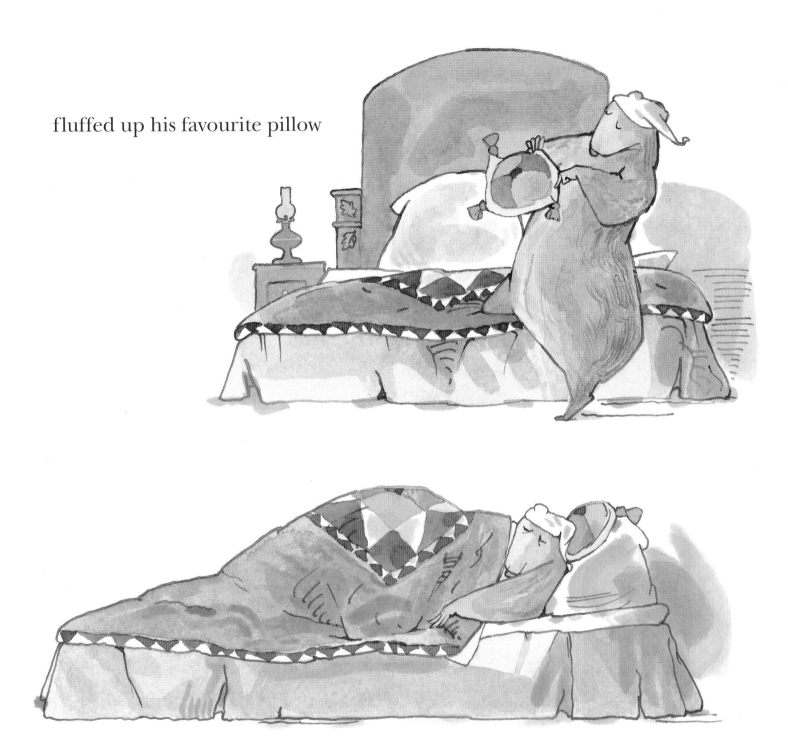

and climbed into bed. It was very, very quiet. He closed his eyes.

Bristle, bristle, bristle. Bear heard a noise. It was Mouse, brushing his teeth.

"Ahem!" Bear cleared his throat in a reminding sort of way.

"Most sorry," said Mouse.

Bear closed his eyes again.

"*Humm, hum-pa-pummmmm,*" Mouse hummed while he put on his nightshirt. "*Pa-pummmmmm.*"

"Absolute quiet…" muttered Bear most patiently.

"Yes, indeed," said Mouse.

Creak, squeak, rattle went Mouse's bed as he hopped in.

Bear jammed his pillow over his ears, gritted his teeth and closed his eyes.

He was just about to drift off when…

"Goodnight, Bear," Mouse called softly.

Bear tried to pretend he was asleep.

"Goodnight," Mouse called a little louder.

"My ears are highly sensitive," cried Bear.

"How interesting," Mouse said.

"Can you hear this?" Mouse mumbled into his pillow.

"Yes!"

"Amazing. How about this?"

Mouse said from under his pillow.

"Quiet!"

Mouse slipped under his blankets, crawled to the bottom of his bed and whispered,

"Can you hear—"

"Silence!" Bear roared.

Mouse slid from his bed, went into the wardrobe, closed the door and said in the tiniest possible voice into the furthest, darkest, teeniest possible corner of the wardrobe, "Surely, you can't—"

"Will this torment never cease?" wailed Bear.

"Sorry, Bear. Goodnight, Bear," whispered Mouse, tiptoeing back
to bed as quiet as a … well, you know.

Bear fluffed up his favourite pillow, adjusted his nightcap and waited.

But there was no sound from Mouse. At last it was quiet.

Very, very quiet.

Bear heard a shuffling sound. "Mouse, is that you?"

No answer.

Bear heard a *crick, crick, crick* on the floorboards.

"I know it's you."

No answer.

"You can't fool me," Bear growled, but he didn't sound very certain.

Bear heard a low moaning noise.

"Mouse?"

Silence.

Bear was sure something was rustling on the floor.

"MOUSE!" he cried. "Wake up!"

Mouse stumbled out of bed, small and grey and sleepy-eyed.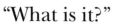

"What is it?"

But Bear couldn't see any rustly, moany sort of thing in his room.

His room looked pretty much like it always looked.

"Nothing," lied Bear, still clutching his blanket to his chin.

"I must have been talking in my sleep."

Bear chuckled. But he sounded rather quavery.

"Ahhhh," said Mouse with a glance at Bear.

"Could I peep under your bed?" asked Mouse. "Sometimes I like to check for … things, you know."

"Well, if you insist," said Bear.

"Nothing," said Mouse from under the bed.

"You'll want to check behind the curtains, I suppose," Bear said.

"All clear," declared Mouse a moment later.

"You'd better check the wardrobe," suggested Bear. "Then you won't be the least bit nervous."

Mouse came out of the wardrobe, dusting his paws.

"Not a thing. Thank you, Bear. Goodnight."

"Wait!" said Bear.

"You'll want a bedtime story, I expect," said Bear. "For your nerves."

"For my nerves?" said Mouse. "Oh, indeed. I'm quite shaken."

Then, with an eager flick of his tail, he settled on Bear's favourite pillow.

And Bear told him all about the adventures of the Brave Strong Bear and
the Very Frightened Little Mouse.

Soon Bear began to yawn.

Mouse yawned, too.

"Goodnight, Bear," said Mouse.

"Goodnight, Mouuuuzzzz," mumbled Bear.

Then Bear began to snore ... LOUDLY.

But Mouse just smiled.

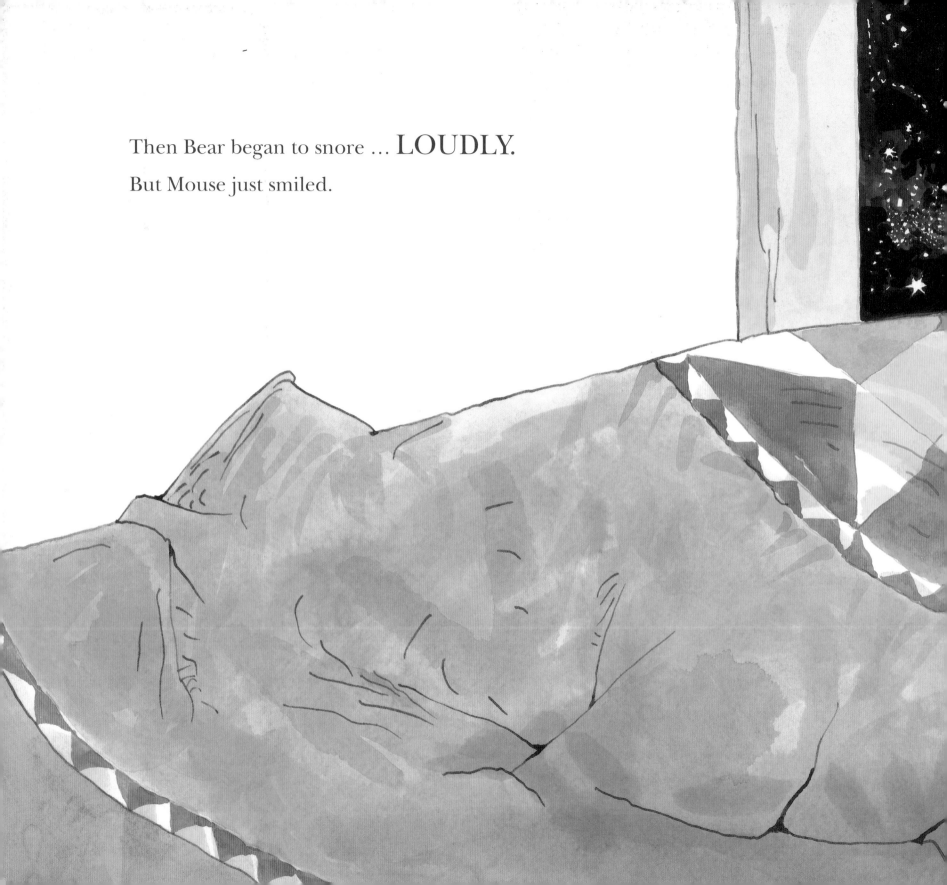

And soon Mouse and Bear were fast asleep.

Shhhhhhhhhh...